Lola the Bear

Lola
the Bear

TRUDE DE JONG

with illustrations by Georgien Overwater

translated by Patricia Crampton

ff

faber and faber

LONDON · BOSTON

First published in Great Britain in 1992
by Faber and Faber Limited
3 Queen Square London WC1N 3AU
Originally published in the Dutch language in 1987
by Sjaloom, Postbus 1895, 1000 BW, Amsterdam, The Netherlands

Photoset by Parker Typesetting Service, Leicester
Printed in England by Clays Ltd St Ives Plc

Trude de Jong is hereby identified as author of this work and
Patricia Crampton as translator in accordance with Section 77
of the Copyright, Designs and Patents Act 1988

A CIP record for this book is available from the British
Library

ISBN 0–571–16236–3

2 4 6 8 10 9 7 5 3 1

For Kohinoor

Contents

 *Noor's Birthday*

It was Noor's birthday. She was five years old.
She had had lots of presents: a doll, rainbow
boots, a painting book and some felt-tipped
pens . . .

Aunt Marian arrived to see her.

'Many happy returns,' she said, giving Noor
a bulky parcel. Noor tore off the wrapping
paper and saw a big bear. It had light-brown fur
and brown eyes and it was wearing a yellow
dress with red spots. So it must be a girl bear.

'Don't you think she's beautiful?' said Aunt
Marian.

'Yes,' said Noor, who was thinking: I'd rather
have a panda. But she did not like to say so.

When her birthday was over, Noor's dad took
her up to bed. They had taken all the presents
up to her bedroom together.

The new doll lay in bed beside Noor.

'Sleep well, sweetheart,' said Dad. He gave
her a big kiss and left the room.

'Sleep well, Josephina Katherina,' said Noor
to her doll. The doll was called after Noor's
mother. She had sent the doll from Australia,
where she had been living with another man for

1

two years now.

But the doll was already asleep, so she said nothing.

'Sleep well, Bear,' said Noor. The bear was sitting on her own with her back against the wall.

'Sleep tight!' Noor called again.

The bear said nothing.

Noor climbed out of bed and went over to her.

'Why don't you say anything? Are you deaf, or something?'

'I'm not saying anything, because you don't like me,' said the bear. 'You'd rather have a panda. All the children are crazy about those wretched pandas!'

Noor's cheeks turned red.

'Not at all,' she said quickly. 'I think you're absolutely lovely!'

'So why can't I come into your bed with you?' asked the bear.

'Come on, then!' Noor picked up the bear and went back to bed.

'Do you always keep your dress on in bed?' asked the bear.

'No, of course not!'

'Then why should I?' asked the bear.

Noor took the bear's dress off. Then she put her arms round the bear and her head on the bear's chest.

'You're nice and soft, Bear,' she said happily.

'My name's not Bear, it's Lola!'

'Sleep well, Lola!' said Noor. She took a peep at the new doll, but luckily the doll was asleep, so she could not be jealous.

'Good kip, Noor!' growled Lola.

Noor did not hear her. She was asleep already.

Where Lola Came From

Lola the bear was sitting on Noor's lap. 'Come on, Lola,' said Noor, 'tell me where you lived when you were a little bear.'

'In Veluwe national park,' said Lola.

'But there aren't any bears in the Netherlands!'

'Oh, all right, so there aren't any bears in the Netherlands. I won't say any more.'

'I do believe you, Lola, go on, tell me more,' coaxed Noor. 'Did you have any brothers or sisters?'

'Two brothers and two sisters,' said Lola. 'Their names are Gazelle, Vondel, Miep and Geyser. They live in a cave with our father and mother.'

'Why don't you live there any more?'

'Well, one day Geyser and I were crossing the Uddel Meadows when we met a man. "Wow!"

he said. "What lovely bears! I'm going to make a bear film, with you two as the stars."

'"Not me," said Geyser.

'"You'll be famous!" cried the man. "You'll get three van-loads every day: one of gold, one of honey and one of letters from bears who are

in love with you. Well?"

'"No!" said Geyser.

'But I said: "I'll come, Mister!"'

'That's what I'd have done too!' said Noor.

'So I went with the man. I thought we were going to the film studio to make a beautiful film, but it was all a cheat. He sold me to a toy shop in Uddel!'

'Poor Lola,' said Noor. 'Do you want to go back to your family?' She was a bit worried that Lola might say yes.

Lola thought it over.

Then she said: 'No, I'll stay with you. But we'll go to Veluwe together in the summer holidays to see my family.'

'That's all right then,' said Noor happily.

Lola-Soup

Noor and Lola were sitting side by side on the sofa, looking at a book together.

Then Noor heard a sound:

rumblerumblerumble.

'Did you hear that, Lola? There's going to be a storm!'

'Oh no, that's my tummy,' growled Lola. 'I'm hungry. I want to eat. NOW!'

'Would you like a peanut butter sandwich?'

'Peanut butter's horrible!' cried Lola. 'Take me to the kitchen and we'll make some Lola-soup.'

Noor put Lola on the draining-board where she could see everything.

'Get a big pan and fill it with hot water,' said Lola.

Noor held a saucepan under the tap. Then she put the heavy pan down beside Lola on the draining-board.

'What else shall I put in it?'

'One packet of butter,' said Lola. 'Three pawfuls of sugar and three pawfuls of flour. One paw is a teacupful.'

Noor poured the sugar, butter and flour into

the saucepan.

'Now give it a good stir!' said Lola.

But the butter would not melt properly.

'Doesn't matter,' said Lola. 'Now a dash of lemonade syrup, a pawful of porridge oats and two rusks. You have to break up the rusks.'

'And now?' Noor wiped her hands on her jumper.

'Half a packet of custard powder . . . and last of all, a pot of chocolate spread.'

'A whole pot?' asked Noor.

'Of course, my girl,' said Lola, 'otherwise it won't be real Lola-soup. Can I have a taste?'

Noor poured the custard powder and chocolate spread into the saucepan. Then she gave Lola a spoonful of soup.

'Wonderful!' cried Lola. She stuck her nose in the saucepan and drank.

Noor tried a spoonful of soup as well.

'Lola-soup is the most delicious soup in the world!' she said.

Dad came into the kitchen, looking very worried about something.

'Come and have some soup, Dad,' said Noor. 'Lola has nearly finished it all up.'

Dad made a face, but he took a spoonful.

'Good, isn't it? Me and Lola made it ourselves!'

'Oh yes, fine, mm,' muttered Dad.

'Lola wants to know if we can make some more soup,' said Noor.

'NO!' shouted Dad.

Noor and Lola looked at each other in surprise. What was wrong with him? Had the Lola-soup made him feel sick?

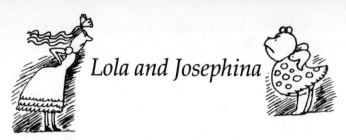

Lola and Josephina

Lola Bear and Josephina Doll were sitting side by side on the seat by the sandpit.

'I haven't got enough room' said Josephina. 'Move your fat bottom, Bear!'

'Fat bottom? Me?' Lola gave Josephina a shove with her paw.

'Oh, do stop squabbling, you two!' said Noor crossly. She sat down between Lola and Josephina. They won't be able to quarrel now, she thought.

'I say, Noor,' said Lola, 'Micky's got a doll with a cassette in its back. It can sing all sorts of nice songs.'

'Yes, I've heard it,' said Noor.

'Perhaps Micky would like to exchange his doll for this one. All this stupid doll can say is Mamma. Mam-ma. Mam-ma!' Lola mimicked.

Josephina stuck her pink nose in the air.

'Noor,' she said, 'I'm so sorry for you, not being able to take that bear out with you. She drops the teacups, eats all the biscuits – and the way she smacks her lips . . . !'

Lola jumped over Noor, grabbed the doll by the neck and growled. Josephina pinched Lola's tummy with her hard doll's fingers. They rolled off the seat, fighting, and fell straight into a puddle of water.

'My dress is wet!' cried Josephina.

'I'm bleeding!' screamed Lola. 'Ring for the ambulance!'

Noor laughed. 'You've just got your head wet in the puddle, silly bear!'

She sat the bear and the doll on the bench in the sun.

'When you are dry you can play in the sandpit,' she said.

Lola and Josephina watched Noor, who was digging a deep hole in the sand.

Lola yawned. Josephina straightened her muddy skirt.

'Hey, Josie,' said Lola.

'My name is Jo-se-phina Ka-the-rina,' said the doll.

'That's too hard for me,' said Lola. 'Listen, Josie, are you bored? I am.'

'Yes!'

'Let's be good again, all right?'

An Accident

'There'll soon be trouble,' said Dad, when he saw Noor and Lola racing up and down the room. 'Off you go, outside!'

'No! It's much more fun in here,' said Noor.

'I can't read with all this going on,' said Dad.

'Don't read then!' shouted Lola. She picked up a tennis ball and threw it to Noor.

A beautiful lamp hung above the table. The shade had a pattern of ships at sea, painted by hand a hundred years ago. The beautiful old lamp was now lying on the table in a hundred fragments. Lola had hit it with the tennis ball.

Dad and Noor stood looking at the broken glass.

'What a shame, Dad,' said Noor. 'You'll have to buy a new one.'

'Impossible,' said Dad, 'those old lamps are very rare. This one belonged to Grandma.' Dad was looking really angry now. 'I told you to play outdoors, didn't I? Who threw a ball in this room?'

'Lola. Lola did it,' said Noor.

'That wretched bear!' shouted Dad. 'That bear's driving me mad. I shall smack her bottom. Where is she?'

But Lola was nowhere to be seen. Not under the table, not behind the seat and not behind the curtains.

So Dad got the dustpan and brush and swept up the glass. He ran out to the kitchen with it,

swearing. Noor searched in her room, under her bed and in her cupboard.

'Lola has gone!' she said.

'Peace at last,' said Dad. 'Hip hip hurrah!'

But Noor began to cry. Dad put his arm round her.

'Don't cry for that bear,' he said. 'She always makes a mess, she always knows best and she shouts at the top of her voice. We'll buy another bear. A little bear which is always sweet and talks quietly.'

'I want Lola!'

'She's sure to come back.'

'No!' cried Noor, 'she won't dare to. You're too cross with her.'

'Of course I'm cross. She smashed my lamp.'

'She's really sorry, Dad,' said Noor, 'and tomorrow we'll make you a new lamp. Shall I paint some bears on the shade?'

'NO!'

'Bottles of beer, then?'

'That's a better idea,' said Dad. He was laughing again now. He took Noor up to bed.

'Sleep well,' he said, and went away.

Noor snuggled down deep under the covers. Suddenly her toes felt something soft.

'Tee hee hee! You're tickling me,' said a gruff voice.

'Lola!'

Noor pulled Lola up from under the duvet and kissed her pale-brown cheeks.

'Found a good hiding-place, didn't I?' said Lola. 'Is Aloysius still cross?'

Aloysius was Noor's father's name.

'You must tell him you're sorry,' said Noor. 'He's still a little bit angry.'

'Sorry? What do you mean?' cried Lola. 'After all, I didn't do it on purpose!'

Marshmallows

'Can we have something nice to eat, too, Dad?' said Noor. She was in the supermarket with Lola and Dad, and she was looking at the shopping trolley. All the things in it were boring: a sliced brown loaf, a carton of milk and a packet of coffee.

Dad picked up a roll of wholemeal biscuits.

'Oh no, not those boring biscuits again!' said Lola.

'Can I have this?' asked Noor, picking up a bag of pink and white marshmallows and putting it in the trolley.

'No,' said Dad, 'you've had enough treats for today.'

'We've only had one ice lolly!' cried Lola. What a pity Dad didn't understand bear language.

He put the sweets back on the shelf and walked on.

Noor thought fast. Should she start screeching or yelling? That sometimes helped . . .

'Take the marshmallows with you,' said Lola in her low, growly voice.

17

'What do you mean?' asked Noor.

'Take the bag and stuff it under your jumper.'

Noor stuffed the marshmallows under her jumper and squeezed Lola to her chest. With her arms round Lola and the marshmallows she followed Dad, who had just finished paying. They left the shop.

Dad stopped to look at a bookshop window display.

'Get the marshmallows out!' growled Lola.

Noor took the bag out from under her jumper and tore it open. She crammed her mouth full of marshmallow.

Dad turned round. 'How in heaven's name did you get hold of that?' he asked.

'Just took it,' said Noor, her mouth full. 'Lola wanted me to take it.'

'And did Lola pay for it?' asked Dad.

'Of course not. Lola doesn't have any money!'

'Lola is a bear,' said Dad, 'and bears don't know that you have to pay at a shop. But you know, don't you?'

'I just didn't think,' whispered Noor.

'Now you will have to pay for the sweets out of the money in your piggy-bank,' said Dad.

'But I don't dare go into the shop, Dad. They'll say Lola's a thief and call the police, and they'll shut Lola up in prison!'

'I shall bite the policemen's bottoms,' said Lola.

'I'll go back to the shop with you,' said Dad. 'We'll pay together and they won't call the police, you'll see. All right?'

'Yes,' said Noor.

But Lola said:

'Pay! How ridiculous!'

A Nasty Meal

Noor, Lola and Dad were sitting at the table.
There were three pans on the table: one with
potatoes in it, one with beans and one with
mince and cabbage.

Dad ladled out the potatoes. One potato fell
on the table. Dad picked it up in his fingers and
shouted: 'Ow!' He slapped the potato on to his
plate.

'Ha ha!' laughed Lola.

'Be quiet, bear!' said Noor.

She took a mouthful of mince. The mince was
tough.

'This mince tastes of soap,' said Lola. 'I'm not
hungry any more.'

She spoke loudly, but luckily Dad did not
hear her.

'Why are you playing with your food?' he
asked Noor.

Noor took a forkful of beans.

'The beans have got those hard stringy bits in
them,' said Lola. 'Nasty, aren't they?'

Noor spat out the beans.

'What's this?' cried Dad. 'That's right, just
spit it out! I've spent hours standing in the

kitchen, trying to cook a healthy meal, and madam sits there, pulling a long face!'

If Dad was to be believed, Noor had a face as long as an elephant's trunk.

'Lola doesn't like it either,' said Noor.

'Go to your room!' roared Dad, 'and take that stupid bear with you!'

'You don't have to shout!' cried Noor. She picked Lola up and ran to her room. She lay on her bed with her head on Lola's tummy. Lola's dress was soon quite wet with tears.

Lola hugged Noor's head in her paws.

'Bad man,' she growled.

Then they heard Dad coming upstairs. He sat on the edge of the bed and put his arms round Noor and Lola together.

'I'm sorry, Noor,' he said. 'I've been in a bad mood all day because my drawing hasn't worked. I shouldn't have shouted at you like that. And the meal *was* horrible.'

He gave Noor a kiss.

'How about Lola?' said Noor.

Dad gave Lola a kiss too.

'I don't think it's at all nice when you shout at me like that,' said Noor. 'But luckily I've got a cry-bear.'

'A cry-bear?'

'When I have to cry I hug Lola,' said Noor. 'Right, Lola?' Lola gave her a wink.

'Would you like chocolate mousse?' asked Dad.

Lola whispered something in Noor's ear and Noor laughed.

'Only chocolate mousse with lots of whipped cream,' she said.

 *Beriberi*

'Noor!' called Lola hoarsely.
  Noor was still asleep.
  'Noor! Wake up!'
  Noor opened her eyes.
  'Huh?' she said.
  'Help!'
  Noor sat straight up in bed.
  'Lola! What is it?'

  She looked across at the little bed which she
had made herself, where Lola slept under an
eiderdown with roses on it.
  Lola had pulled the eiderdown right over her

head. Noor drew it down gently . . .

Lola's brown eyes were glittering and her teeth were chattering.

'Are you frightened?'

'Of course not,' said Lola, through chattering teeth. 'I've got beriberi.'

'What's that?'

'A very dangerous illness,' said Lola. 'Call the doctor, quick!'

'I'll have to take your temperature first,' said Noor. 'Will you stay in bed?'

'I was just about to fly to America!' cried Lola, 'or take a steamer to Spain . . . ! Of course I'll stay in bed, I'm really ill, aren't I!'

Noor picked up the thermometer and popped it under Lola's arm.

The line inside the thermometer rushed up to over 42 degrees. That was as high as it could go.

'I'll ring the doctor straight away,' said Noor.

'Yes,' groaned Lola, 'quickly, I'm dying!'

The vet's telephone number was on a card on the peg-board.

Noor rang the number.

24

'My bear's got beriberi,' she said. 'What shall I do?'

'Well, that's not too bad,' said the vet, whose name was Gerda, 'but bears always think it's very dangerous. Put your bear out in the sunshine and give her two pounds of raw sprouts. She'll get better straight away. Goodbye!'

'Thank you very much,' said Noor. 'Lola, the doctor says you've got to go outside.'

'No,' cried Lola, 'I want to stay indoors!'

But Noor put the rose eiderdown round Lola's shoulders and carried her outside. She sat Lola down on the balcony in the sunshine.

'Now I'm going to buy you two pounds of sprouts,' she said.

'What?' screamed Lola. 'Sprouts? Is that what the stupid doctor said? What I need is two pounds of boiled sweets, do you hear? Two pounds of boiled sweets!'

'If you can shout like that you're better already,' said Noor. She went to the kitchen and fetched a handful of sprouts and a handful of sweets. Lola ate up all the sweets, smacking her lips, but she spat the sprouts out over the balcony.

'You're supposed to eat them up, Lola!'

'Hip hip hurrah!' cried Lola. 'I'm better! The beriberi has gone to another bear!'

To another bear? Or perhaps to a child?

All at once Noor began to feel a little bit shivery . . .

In Love

The sun was shining. It was real sandpit
weather today. Noor got her bucket and spade
and plastic moulds and went downstairs with
Lola under her arm.

Christian from the flat below was there too.
He was already in the sandpit. Noor put Lola
down on the sand.

'Do you want whipped cream or chocolate
cake?' she asked. Lola said nothing.

'Lola! Say something!'

'Noor,' whispered Lola, 'who is that?'

'Christian.'

'No, silly goose, there!' said Lola, pointing. A
brown toy bear was sitting on the seat.

'That's Christian's bear.'

'Put me beside him!' Lola hissed.

'I was going to play with you,' said Noor.

'Do as I say, girl. Take me to that handsome
bear at once!'

27

Noor put Lola on the seat beside Christian's bear.

'Hallo-o-o. . .' said Lola.

'Good morning, miss,' said the bear.

Noor ran back to the sandpit and played with Christian all afternoon without once looking at Lola.

At half-past five Dad called them in to eat.

Noor went over to the seat where the bears were talking.

'Coming, Lola?'

'Already?'

'Yes.' Noor picked Lola up.

'Goodbye, Romeo,' Lola called.

'Adieu!' said the bear in a deep, growly voice.

'Did you have fun?' asked Noor, as they ran home.

'Fun? Fun? It was fantastic!' cried Lola. 'His real name is Harry, but he likes to be called Romeo. We kissed each other at least seventy-five times, didn't you see?'

'No.'

'I'm in love!' cried Lola. 'We've arranged to meet by the sandpit at three-thirty tomorrow. Ring up Christian and tell him!'

Noor laughed. When she got in she rang up Christian straight away. Lola wanted to talk to Romeo on the telephone.

'So bears have to telephone nowadays as well!' said Dad. 'Crazy, eh?'

'Yes,' said Noor. 'Lola is crazy. Crazy about Romeo.'

Buying Shoes

Dad, Noor and Lola were walking into town. They were going to buy shoes, new shoes for Noor. They did that twice a year, mostly in the sales, when the expensive children's shoes were a little cheaper.

They went into the first shoe shop they came to. The children's shoes in the sale were arranged on the floor.

'Can I help you?' asked a saleswoman.

'I want a pair of shoes for my daughter. Not sandals, because it's nearly autumn.'

'Luckily it's only June now, sir. Shall I measure the young lady's foot?'

Noor put her foot in a sort of box and the

saleswoman moved the sides of the box in until they touched it.

'Length thirty-two, width three,' she said. 'Let's see what we've got.'

She picked up a pair of red shoes with straps.

'How do you like these?'

'Disgusting!' cried Lola.

'No,' said Noor.

'Don't you like red? Here's a blue pair with velcro fastenings.'

'Those are boy's shoes. I want red shoes with golden heels, like Elvira's.'

'If Elvira's mother wants Elvira to get bad feet, that's up to Elvira's mother,' said Dad.

'Don't you think these are pretty?' asked the saleswoman, showing Noor a pair of white shoes. They were just like a nurse's shoes.

'Mwah,' said Noor.

'Try these on,' said the saleswoman.

Noor tried the monsters on, and then she had to walk up and down in them. Lola was doubled up with laughter.

'How do they fit?' asked the saleswoman.

'They're too small,' said Noor.

'Oh, we've got them in a larger size.'

'No, they're too big!'

'That's good. You can grow into them,' said Dad. 'We'll take them.'

Noor looked at Lola, who shook her head vigorously. 'Don't have them!'

There was only one thing Noor could do: she set up a hideous howl.

'I don't want those shoes!' she sobbed.

'But you've got to have shoes,' said Dad.

'I'll go around in bare feet!'

'Always the same kerfuffle,' said Dad. His face had gone red because everyone was looking at them. 'What *do* you want?'

Noor stopped crying and pointed to a pair of gym shoes with Snoopy on them.

'Those are not in the sale,' said the saleswoman.

'Gym shoes are bad for your feet, too,' said Dad.

Noor started snivelling again.

When they came out of the shop a few minutes later Noor was wearing her new gym shoes.

'Thanks, Dad,' she said, 'they fit beautifully! Can we go to a toy shop now? Lola wants some new shoes too.'

'NO!' said Dad.

Homesickness

Noor and Lola were staying the night with
Christian and his bear Romeo. They had eaten
pancakes, watched TV, and Christian's mother
had read them a story. Now the four of them
were lying cosily side by side in bed. But Noor
was not feeling too good.

'My tummy hurts,' she said.
'Probably ate too many pancakes,' said
Christian.
'No. I feel so funny. Do you think I'm ill?'
'You're homesick,' said Lola.
'What's that?'
'You feel sick because you want to go home.'
'Yes! I want to go back to Dad!'

34

'No, no!' shouted Christian and Romeo, 'you stay. Mum's letting us make Lola-soup tomorrow!'

'I was homesick once,' said Romeo the bear, in his deep growly voice.

'You were?' said Lola, surprised.

'Well? Everyone gets homesick sometimes.'

'Yes,' said Lola, 'I'd like to see my father and mother again too. Tell us about it, Romeo.'

'One evening Christian and I went out in his father's boat. He's a fisherman, as you know. A storm got up, the waves were as tall as blocks of flats, and Christian was sick.'

'Not true!' cried Christian. 'I just felt a little bit wobbly, that's all!'

'Suddenly a huge wave hit us, and I fell overboard. The water was icy-cold. There you go, Romeo, I thought, it's all up with you! At that moment I saw a door floating by. It was the cabin door. I climbed on to it at once.'

'How clever you are!' said Lola.

'I know, Lola-doll! Well then, I was floating along. The boat was nowhere to be seen. The storm died down and I lay on my back on the

door, gazing at the moon and stars. I hadn't had a bite to eat, nothing but sea-water to drink, but I felt happy. Then the sun came up and I was saved by a helicopter . . .'

'Yes, otherwise you wouldn't be here now!'

'Excuse me, Lola, may I go on? That evening I lay exhausted in this wonderful, soft bed, safe with Christian. But I could not sleep. Do you know why? I was missing my door.'

Noor, Lola and Christian giggled.

'What are you laughing about?' Romeo asked.

'Funny sort of homesickness,' said Christian.

'Maybe. But do you know what I do when I can't sleep? I imagine I'm lying on that door, bobbing up and down on the waves. You try it!'

Noor, Christian and Lola closed their eyes.

'Are you floating comfortably?' asked Christian.

'Mm . . .' said Noor. She was feeling very sleepy.

'I'm seasick. Help!' cried Lola.

'Don't fool about, girl,' said Romeo. 'A little quieter, please. Noor is asleep.'

The New Dress

'Want to come to the sandpit?' Noor asked Lola. 'Christian and his bear Romeo are coming.'

'No,' said Lola.

'No? Aren't you in love with Romeo any more?'

'Terribly. But I've got nothing to wear.'

'You've got a beautiful yellow dress with red spots on.'

'*You've got a beautiful yellow dress with red spots on,*' Lola mimicked Noor. 'Always the same old dress. I want a new dress!'

'I can't make you a new dress,' said Noor, 'but Dad can.'

She tucked Lola under her arm and went to find Dad. He was busy working on a drawing.

'Dad, will you make Lola a new dress?' she asked him.

'I've never done that before,' said Dad.

'Do try, Dad! Romeo Bear is coming to the sandpit and Lola would like to have a new dress.'

Dad stood up, sighing. He hunted through a dustbin-bag full of old clothes and pulled out an old flowery blouse of Noor's.

38

'Do you like this?'

'Lola says she does,' said Noor.

Dad got some scissors and cut two pieces out of the blouse.

'It's going to be a pinafore frock,' he said. 'That's the easiest.'

He sewed the two pieces together with big stitches. He pricked his finger twice, but Lola and Noor did not laugh.

As soon as the pinafore frock was finished, Noor tried it on Lola.

'Good, eh? Beautiful, isn't it?' said Dad proudly.

'Dad,' said Noor, 'Lola says she doesn't think the pinafore is very beautiful. She says she would rather wear her old dress.'

'Oh yes?' said Dad.

'Lola thinks it's very clever of you, you see,' said Noor, 'but she says she thinks you need a bit of practice first.'

'Is that what she says!' Dad was looking really cross.

Noor ran out of the room with Lola tucked under her arm. She forgot to take Lola's old dress, so Lola had to go to the sandpit in her new dress, after all. If only Romeo still thought her beautiful . . .

In Hospital 1

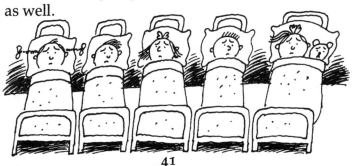

Noor was not allowed anything to eat that morning. She was in bed, and in hospital. Lola was tucked in beside her and Dad was sitting on the edge of the bed. There were five other children lying in bed in the big ward. Noor had the nicest bed, by the window, where she could watch the trains going by.

'I wish I was in the train,' said Lola.

'Why?'

'Hospitals are nasty!'

'Don't make a fuss,' said Noor. 'I'm having the operation, not you.'

'Coming with me?' asked Irma. Irma was a very nice lady. She had told the children exactly what was going to happen. All the children were going to have their tonsils out, and some of them were going to have their adenoids out as well.

'It's time for that prick now!'

'Ooeeeee . . .' sighed Lola.

Irma and Dad pushed Noor's bed-on-wheels into a little room. Nurse Kees put Noor into a green operating gown and drew a yellow sun on her leg. He gave her the injection in the middle of the sun and it hardly hurt at all. Dad was holding Noor's hand tightly.

Lola put her paws over her eyes.

Nurse Kees gave Noor a pill.

'It will help the pain in your throat,' he explained.

'Horrible,' muttered Lola.

Noor was wheeled back to the ward, where she had to wait for another nurse.

The nurse, Irma and Dad walked down the passage with Noor in her bed. Dad was not allowed to come in the lift. He gave Noor several big kisses.

'See you in ten minutes,' he said.

'As soon as that?' said Lola.

'Bye, Dad,' said Noor, very quietly.

They took the lift to the first floor, where the operating theatre was.

Irma had to go back to the other children.

43

'Bye-bye, Noor,' she said cheerfully. 'I'll come back and get you soon.'

'Bye,' whispered Noor.

The nurse wheeled Noor into the operating theatre. The doctors had green caps on their heads and paper masks over their mouths. There was a huge lamp over a table.

'Hallo, Noor,' said one of the doctors. Noor said nothing. She suddenly felt awful and hoped she wasn't going to be sick.

Lola whispered something in Noor's ear.

'Doctor,' said Noor, 'Lola wants an operation too. We think it would be cosier.'

The doctor laughed. 'Fine,' she said, 'I'll do you both at the same time.'

Noor and Lola had to sit on the nurse's lap. A green sheet was folded round them and a black cap was put on Noor's nose. Irma had told them that the sleeping gas came out of the cap. The sleeping gas smelled horrible.

'Now me!' cried Lola. Noor fell asleep.

In Hospital 2

'Noor! Noor!' she heard someone calling. Noor opened her eyes. She was lying in a small room and the nurse was standing beside her bed with a glass of lemonade.

'Have a drink,' she said.

Swallowing hurt a lot. Noor grabbed Lola.

'Careful!' said Lola. 'My throat! That doctor there is not a doctor, she's a butcher!'

'The pain will be less in an hour,' said the nurse.

Noor saw Irma's cheerful face again.

'It's all over,' she said. 'You may find that your nose or your throat bleeds a little, but don't be frightened. It happens. Soon you'll be eating delicious water ices.'

Irma and the nurse wheeled Noor's bed out of the lift.

Dad was waiting, looking a little pale.

'Hallo Noor, hallo darling,' he said. 'How goes it?'

'Sore throat,' whispered Noor. She was very glad the operation was over.

'Lola had an operation, too,' said the nurse.

'Well well! That Lola!' said Dad.

'Bring on the water ices!' said Lola.

And the water ices came, as many as they wanted. What a pity that swallowing hurt so much. Noor's ears hurt as well. Irma pressed a flannel against them and the pain went away.

Dad read aloud to Noor and Lola. He was allowed to stay with them all day. At half-past seven Noor and Lola had to go to sleep and it was time for Dad to leave.

'I'll come and pick you up at nine o'clock tomorrow morning,' he said. 'Goodbye, brave girls!'

Noor and Lola fell asleep at once.

Next morning Irma asked: 'How is your throat?'

'It still hurts a bit,' said Noor, 'but not as much as yesterday.' Lola whispered something in Noor's ear.

'Lola's throat is quite better,' said Noor, 'and she says she wants to be a doctor.'

'So are you going to stay here in hospital, Lola?' asked Irma.

'NO!' shouted Lola.

'She's coming home with me now, Irma. Later, she says.'

'Right you are, Doctor Lola!' said Irma. 'Look, there's Dad, come to take you home!'

Madurodam

One day Noor, Lola and Dad went by train to The Hague to visit the miniature town of Madurodam. Outside the railway station they took the tram.

'Isn't it hot,' sighed Lola. 'I want a drink!'

'When will we be there, Dad?' asked Noor. 'Lola's thirsty, and so am I.'

'We'll be there soon.' Dad wiped his forehead with a big red handkerchief.

At last they reached Madurodam. There was a long queue at the ticket office.

'Get a move on!' shouted Lola. It did not help.

'It's almost our turn now,' said Dad. 'It's such

fun for me to see Madurodam again. I was
brought here myself twenty-five years ago.'

Dad bought two tickets, because bears are
allowed in for nothing.

Noor saw little houses, churches and
windmills everywhere. Real trains were
running along the tracks and boats were sailing
down a river.

'Look, that is Utrecht Cathedral,' said Dad –
but of course, Noor and Lola knew that already!

'And there is the airport.' Dad was moving off to look at it, but Noor was kneeling down in front of one of the houses. She gave the front door a tug but it would not open. She looked in through a window.

'See anything?' asked Lola.

'Nothing. Perhaps they've gone shopping. I'll look in the next-door houses.'

At the next house Noor knocked on the door and called: 'Come on out!'

'Are you deaf?' shouted Lola.

'They don't want to come out, Lola!'

'They're all down at the beach in this weather, I expect,' said Lola.

'What are you talking about?' asked Dad. 'Who is it that won't come out?'

'The people who live here, of course,' said Noor.

Dad looked quite blank. 'People?'

'Yes. Little people live here, don't they?

That's what the houses are for.'

Dad laughed. 'Nobody lives here,' he said.

'Not even a bear?' asked Lola.

'Then what did they build this town for?' asked Noor.

'They just did. For fun,' said Dad.

Noor looked cross.

'Would you like to live here?' said Dad. 'With all these people pressing their noses against your window and staring in?'

'Funny if you were sitting on the lav!' said Lola. Noor thought about it.

'No,' she said, 'but then why don't they make proper dolls' houses, with real chairs and tables for me to play with?'

'Good idea. We'll write a letter to the Mayor of Madurodam,' said Dad.

'Where does he live?' Noor looked around. She was eager to see the tiny mayor.

'No, he doesn't live here,' said Dad. Noor

gave up.

'Shall we go to the beach now?' she asked.

'Something to drink first,' said Dad.

'Aha, at last!' shouted Lola.

 *Sleep*

Noor and Lola were in bed. Lola gave a tremendous yawn.

'Stop that!' cried Noor. 'Now you've made me yawn too.' She yawned until tears ran down her cheeks.

'I'm going to sleep. Sleep well, Lola.'

'Good kip, Noor!'

Noor closed her eyes, but she couldn't sleep. She kept on thinking about Madurodam, the beach at Scheveningen, and the train.

Lola was restless too, tossing and turning all the time.

'Do keep still, Lola!'

'I can't get to sleep.' Lola sighed deeply. 'I'm frightened.'

Noor sat up in bed.

'You're frightened? What of?'

'It's silly, I'm not going to tell,' growled Lola.

'But you can tell me, can't you?'

'Promise you won't laugh?'

'No, honestly, Lola. I promise.'

'Well,' said Lola, 'when I close my eyes it's just as if I'm falling into a deep, dark hole. And then I'm frightened that I might die.'

53

'That's impossible, Lola. You're much too young. You don't die until you're about a hundred.'

'Is that right?' said Lola, in a very small voice. 'But what happens when I'm dead?'

'I don't know either,' said Noor.

'Now I daren't go to sleep, and I'm so tired,' sobbed Lola. Noor hugged her tightly.

'Never mind,' she said, 'I can't sleep either.'

'Why can't you sleep?'

'I keep thinking about Madurodam and Dad asleep on the sand on his towel . . .'

'Oh, yes,' said Lola, 'and then you got your spade . . .'

'That was your idea!'

'Wasn't! And then you scooped up that jellyfish and dumped it on his tummy!'

Noor giggled.

'He jumped up and yelled so loud the whole beach heard him. Fancy a grown-up man being so frightened of a little jellyfish!'

'It was a very big, nasty fat jellyfish, Lola!'

Noor and Lola burst out laughing.

'But your dad is very nice. After that he gave us another ice-cream each.'

'That was good,' said Noor dreamily, 'a great big ice-cream, with cherryade at the bottom, strawberry ice-cream and vanilla ice-cream and whipped cream with nuts . . . What do you call that kind of ice-cream, Lola?'

Lola said nothing. Noor saw that she had fallen asleep, and she was not dead, because she was snoring. When Lola was tired she always snored very loudly. Noor kissed her on the top of her head.

'Sweet dreams, Lola, see you tomorrow!'

Saved

'It's much too warm to go bicycling,' sighed Dad.

'We don't think so,' said Noor. She was sitting in a little seat on the front of the bicycle, with Lola in her arms. 'Lola wants to know if we're there yet.'

'Perhaps you'd like to do the pedalling?'

'Yes!' shouted Noor and Lola.

'On the way home, then. We're there now.'

Dad dismounted, put Noor and Lola down on the ground and picked up a bulging beach-bag. The three of them dragged it through the wood, all the way to the beach. Dad found a quiet spot and unpacked the bag. Noor took out her clothes. She had brought a swimming costume, a blue one, with little Mickey Mouses on it. Poor Lola had to wear some knickers of Noor's. Why didn't they sell any swimming costumes for bears?

'Are you coming into the water, Lola?'

'Will you carry me down to the sea in a towel? I don't want anybody to see my swimming pants,' Lola grumbled.

'Romeo isn't around.'

'Listen,' said Dad, 'you can paddle in the sea up to your bottoms. No further!'

'I know that!' Noor raced down to the sea and unwrapped Lola's towel.

'Hurry up! Everyone's looking!' hissed Lola. Noor ran quickly into the water.

'Can you swim, Lola?'

'Of course I can swim. I swam in Lake Uddel every day. But now I'd like to float.'

Noor put Lola on her back and she bobbed along on the waves.

'Can you float?' shouted Lola.

'Of course I can!' Noor lay down on the water, but the water didn't hold her up. She sank to the bottom. She stood up quickly, coughing and spluttering because of the water in her nose and mouth.

'Call that floating? You looked like a dying dolphin!' called Lola.

'I was diving!' said Noor crossly. I'm going to start swimming lessons tomorrow, she thought to herself.

Lola was singing a sea shanty about high waves, sinking ships and weeping sailors' wives. She had already drifted quite a long way from Noor.

'Lola, come back!' shouted Noor.

Lola stopped singing. She looked round.

'Where's the shore?' she called. 'I want to come back!'

She kicked out vigorously with her paws, but she was drifting further out to sea all the time.

'Save me!' she shrieked, but the swimmers could not hear her. 'HELP!'

Noor had to help her. She ran into the sea. The water came up to her waist, to her chest and then up to her chin. She could almost touch Lola.

'Noor!' shouted Lola.

Noor reached out both arms and jumped. She had to save Lola! The water rushed over her head. Under the water everything was blue and silent. Noor wanted to get out, but there was water everywhere. She could scarcely breathe . . .

Someone gripped her by the shoulders and pulled her out. Dad was holding her in his arms and walking up the beach. He wrapped her in a bathing towel and rubbed her dry.

'Why did you go so far out?' he asked.

'That's why.' Noor held up a sopping-wet Lola. With no pants on.

'Am I dead?' asked Lola weakly. 'Am I in heaven now?'

'No. I saved you,' said Noor proudly.

'That's nice,' said Dad. 'I'm going to exchange that bear for a pit bull terrier this very day!'

But of course he didn't mean it.

Treasure

'Here's your spade,' said Dad. 'Good luck!'

Holding Lola tightly, Noor ran up the beach. A lot of children were waiting, each one with a spade and a greedy look on its face. The parents watched from behind metal fences.

'Do you think it's here, Lola?'

'No, go further on!'

Noor walked on slowly. Suddenly she felt sure: it's here, in this very spot! And Lola also shouted: 'Stop!'

Noor stuck her spade in the sand. This was her place, no other child would be allowed to come here. She put Lola down.

'Get going!' Lola ordered.

But that was not allowed. Mr Wilbert, of Wilbert's Snack Palace, had to give the starting signal. Then the children could start digging.

Wilbert's fat red face shone in the sun. He held up a flag and yelled: 'Everybody ready . . . everybody dig!' All the children began to dig like mad. Sand flew through the air. Noor felt sorry for them. She alone knew where the treasure was. She began to dig energetically.

'Got it yet?' asked Lola.

Noor said nothing. Beads of sweat were trickling down her face, but she just went on digging.

'Hey, Noor, keep it up!' shouted Lola.

Noor was up to her knees in the pit she was digging. She had no time to look at the other children. At any moment her spade might strike the iron lid of the treasure chest!

'Hallo, Noor!'

She brushed the hair off her face and looked up. Dad was standing on the edge of her pit.

That was odd: he wasn't allowed to be there, was he?

'Stop now, Noor. The treasure hunt is over.'

'It can't be. I haven't got the treasure yet!' said Noor.

'One of the boys has found it,' said Dad.

'What!' shouted Lola.

Noor couldn't believe her ears. She looked around. All the children were running down the beach with their spades.

'But it must be here!' she said stubbornly.

Dad was standing in the pit.

'What a lovely deep pit,' he said. 'You certainly did your best.'

'I don't care about the stupid pit!' screamed Noor. 'I want the treasure!'

She threw her spade down furiously and began to cry. Dad put his arm round her.

'It was a rotten treasure,' he said. 'Just a tin with some old waffles from Wilbert's Snack Palace.'

'Oh,' said Noor, disappointed, 'I thought it was going to be a big treasure chest full of gold and silver and necklaces and diamond rings.'

'You mean a real pirate treasure? Do you really think Wilbert would give away a precious treasure like that?'

'Of course not!' cried Lola. 'He sells such mean little bags of chips!'

'You have to find a real treasure for yourself,'

62

said Dad. 'For instance after a big storm, when a ship has gone down. That's when a treasure might be washed up on a quiet beach somewhere.'

'When will there be a storm, Dad?'
Dad looked at the sky.

'See that big grey cloud there? It shouldn't be long now.'

'Fine. We'll go and hunt for real treasure tomorrow,' said Noor.

'And then we'll be stinking rich!' cried Lola.

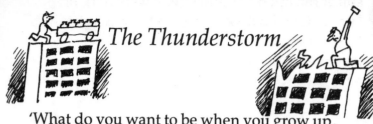

The Thunderstorm

'What do you want to be when you grow up, Lola?' asked Noor.

'Nothing. I'm much too lazy to work,' said Lola.

'I want to be a dentist. Are you afraid of the dentist?'

'No. Go to sleep now.'

'I can't sleep. It's much too hot. I shall buy a drill and a big chair. And I shall be famous because I shall make false teeth with patterns and flowers on them. I shall give Dad a pair of false teeth for nothing when he's old. Do you want some too?'

Lola said nothing. She had gone to sleep, boring thing.

Noor stared at the curtains, which hung quite

still at the open window. They were dark blue and had red boats on them with white sails. At least the boats had found some wind, because they were sailing.

I wish I was in a boat like that, thought Noor, and the wind was blowing, and it was cold enough to make me shiver. Noor shivered. It helped! She really did feel a bit less hot. She put her thumb in her mouth and fell asleep.

Noor was woken by the uproar over her head. It sounded like someone pushing a truckful of clattering bottles just above her. But they couldn't be, because she lived on the top floor. Was somebody repairing the roof? A brilliant flash of lightning lit up the room and there was a loud crash. Noor closed her eyes tightly and pulled the duvet over her head.

'Lola! There's a thunderstorm!'

'Well?' said Lola sleepily. 'Where I lived on the Veluwe, we had them all the time.'

'The lightning will kill us! Daddy!'

Dad didn't hear her. He was asleep, of course. She could still see the lightning, right through her eyelids and the duvet.

'I want to go to Dad!'

'Off you go then!'

'I don't dare!'

It sounded as if men were smashing the house with huge hammers.

'You needn't be frightened as long as I'm with you,' said Lola.

Noor sobbed like a baby.

'Weren't you going to be a famous dentist? A famous dentist is never frightened. She would always be brave enough to run to her dad's bedroom,' said Lola.

'I am a famous dentist and I'm not afraid,'
said Noor bravely. She picked up Lola, pushed
the duvet aside and sat on the edge of her bed.
The thunder had stopped for the time being.

Now! She raced to the door with Lola. The
door stuck. She saw another fearful flash of
lightning and heard a violent crash. 'Help!'
screamed Noor. The door flew open and she

raced down the dark passage. The door to
Dad's room was open. Noor flew across the
room and leapt on to Dad in bed.

'What's happened?' yelled Dad.

'Thunderstorm!' Noor crept under the duvet
and clung to Dad. That way she couldn't see the
lightning and she no longer cared about the
claps of thunder. She was safe in the big bed.
Dad got out the jar of liquorice that he kept
under the bed for emergencies. 'A
thunderstorm is an emergency,' said Dad. 'Can
you hear? It's starting to rain. The

thunderstorm is over.'

The three of them lay in bed, sucking liquorice.

Lola giggled.

'I bet Aloýsius will be needing false teeth quite soon!' she said.

Make-Up

Noor and Lola were sitting at the table, finger-painting.

Suddenly Lola cried: 'Hey, Noor!'

'What is it, Lola?'

'Am I beautiful?'

'You've got a funny face,' said Noor.

'Funny? I don't want to be funny, I want to be beautiful!' shouted Lola.

'You're beautiful too,' said Noor quickly.

'But I want to be more beautiful. And you've got to help me.'

'How?'

'You must make my face really beautiful. With lipstick and things.'

'We haven't got any lipstick,' said Noor.

'Silly! We've got finger-paint, haven't we? Get started!'

'OK.' Noor stuck her finger in the brown paint.

'Shut your eyes.'

Noor made a brown circle round Lola's eyes. Then she filled in the circle with green paint.

'Finished?' asked Lola.

'Nearly.' Noor painted Lola's cheeks pink.

'Hurry up!' said Lola.

'Now the lipstick. Stop talking and keep your lips still for once.' Noor gave Lola a very big red mouth.

before   after

'Ready! You can look in the mirror now,' said Noor. 'What do you think of it?'

'OOWEE-HEE, BEOOTIFUL!!!' shrieked Lola, 'Romeo must see this!'

But first Noor made herself beautiful, too. When she had finished she looked very much like Lola. She only needed two yellow ears to make them look like twins.

Noor and Lola ran to the sandpit. Christian was there with his bear Romeo, whose real name was Harry. 'You two look quite crazy!' said Christian.

'Ho ho ho!' went Romeo, laughing his deep growly laugh. 'An oil painting on paws!'

'Stupid boy!' said Noor, and Lola screamed: 'We're all washed up, Harry, do you hear?'

They went off, feeling very cross. There was

the fruit-and-veg man with his barrow. He
laughed. 'How about a juicy apple?' he said.
'You can have it free, gratis and for nothing.
Because you are so beautiful.'

Lola gave the fruit-and-veg man a big red kiss
on the cheek.

Temper

When Noor came home from school she found Lola sitting on the seat, looking cross.

'Why are you so late?' Lola snarled.

'I had to help Miss Williams clear away.'

'Can't that stupid Williams do it herself? You're out all day, and I'm bored to death!'

'I can't come home at lunchtime, Lola. All the other children stay too.'

'So take me with you!'

'It's not allowed,' said Noor. She didn't want to take Lola to school. Christian had taken his bear to school the other day, and the whole class had laughed at him.

Dad came out of the kitchen with two bowls of mushroom soup.

'Lola is cross because I'm out all day,' said Noor.

'And Aloysius doesn't say a word!' cried Lola.

'You must talk to Lola when I'm not there, Dad.'

'I'll do that,' said Dad. He sat on the seat beside Noor and Lola, and took a book out of his coat pocket.

72

'I found this in the shed,' he said. 'It used to be my favourite book. It's called *Gnometown*.'

'Not going to read to us, is he?' asked Lola.

'I'm going to read to you while you're having your soup.'

'Oh, no,' groaned Lola.

'Hold your tongue!' said Noor.

Dad read: '"One beautiful sunny day, Stuff'n'gulp the gnome was dozing under his toadstool . . ."'

'What's dozing, Dad?'

'He was having a little sleep. "His pointed cap had tipped forward over his nose and his lips were making a peculiar noise: gruh-gruh-gruh . . ."'

'I'm going to sleep too. What a boring story!' sighed Lola.

'"He had had such a gorgeous feast,"' Dad read. '"A dish of cooked acorns, stuffed toadstools and a tulipful of rosehip wine."'

'Disgusting!' cried Lola.

'How could he drink from a tulip?' said Noor. 'The wine would run out, wouldn't it?'

'In this story he can. Just listen. "His tummy was full and round. Stuff'n'gulp the gnome was asleep, when guess who came stealing in? Yes, it was the wicked fox Redbrush who . . ."'

'Dad! Lola wants to know if Redbrush is his first or his second name?'

'His first name, I think. I'll go on reading.'

'Yes, but Dad, Lola wants to know what his second name is.'

'Redbrush Brown. All right? Keep quiet, Lola!'

Noor and Lola giggled.

'"Licking his lips, Redbrush ran towards the sleeping Stuff'n'gulp . . ."'

'Why was he licking his lips?' asked Noor.

'Because he was dying of hunger.'

'What a nasty fox!' Lola shouted.

'"So, licking his lips, Redbrush ran towards the sleeping Stuff'n'gulp and . . ."'

'And gobbled him up in one gulp!' cried Noor and Lola, rolling off the seat with laughter.

Dad slammed the book shut.

'I'm never going to read aloud again!' he said.

'Oh, come on Dad, what happened to the gnome?' said Noor, still spluttering. But Dad picked up the empty soup bowls and went off to the kitchen without a word.

'Now I shall never find out what the gnome's first name was,' giggled Lola. 'Perhaps it was Aloysius.'

Noor was glad that Lola's bad temper had gone. But it was a pity Dad had caught it.

Ming Chi

'No, I'm not going to the sandpit,' said Lola. 'I
NEVER want to see that stupid Romeo again.
And I'm going to call him Harry from now on!'

She was in a bad temper because her
friendship with Romeo the bear was over. Noor
had an idea. She ran down the stairs to the flat
on the first floor. When she came back she was
carrying a large panda bear in her arms. He had
been lent to her by Imre. Imre was only three
weeks old and could do without him for now.

'Lola! Visitor!'

'If it's Harry tell him I'm not at home!' cried
Lola. Then she saw the panda bear, who made a
bow, saying: 'A pleasure to make your
acquaintance, beautiful Cherry Blossom.'

'My name is Lola, goose!'

'My name is Ming Chi, not Goose,' said the
panda.

Noor sat him down next to Lola on the sofa.
She took a pad of paper and some felt-tips and
began to draw at the table, where she could
hear what the two bears were saying to each
other.

'I was born in Hong Kong,' said Ming Chi.

'That is a big, busy metropolis in China.'

'I come from Uddel and it's a much bigger and busier mepoppolip! Did you have a pleasant journey?'

'Alas, no, fair Bud of Spring,' said Ming Chi. 'I travelled with a hundred other pandas,

crowded into a dark space. But the toyshop in Amsterdam was very beautiful. I also made an instructive journey by train from Amsterdam to Utrecht. We travelled past an impressive coffee factory. I would like to visit that one day. Will you come with me, Shining Orchid?'

'I've seen that factory too often already,' said Lola. 'I'd rather go to the funfair. Have you ever been on the switchback ride? I have, often, and I was never frightened. Harry was, of course. Harry wet his pants with fright!'

'You are most brave, fragrant Tiger Lily,' said Ming Chi. 'If I may ask, is Harry by any chance your betrothed?'

'Not any more. I broke the engagement. Two days, seven hours and thirty-four and a half minutes ago.'

Ming Chi sighed with relief. Then he made a dignified speech: 'I am a bear of few words. Will you, sweet Sugar Cane, share my bamboo shoots with me for ever?'

'I don't like bamboo. Give me chips and vinegar every time.'

'I mean, treasured Ivy Tendril, will you marry me?'

Noor held her breath. She hoped Lola would say yes. Then she would have lots of little panda bears later on.

Lola said: 'My heart is broken. Later, perhaps.'

'Poor little Dandelion Flower. May Ming Chi comfort you? Here is a present for you.'

Ming Chi took the bright silk scarf from his neck and gave it to Lola.

'Presents! I'm mad about presents!'

Lola knotted the scarf round her waist.

'I must say farewell, precious Plum Blossom. Imre awaits me. Farewell!'

'Bye!' called Lola. 'And thanks for the scarf, Blooming Stinging Nettle.'

Noor took Ming Chi home. When she came back she asked Lola: 'Well, what did you think of him?'

'You know very well that I think pandas are stupid!' said Lola. But she gave the beautiful Chinese scarf a very satisfied smile.

The Competition

Noor was sitting in the sandpit with Lola and Ming Chi when Christian arrived with Romeo Bear under his arm.

'Oo-er!' said Christian. 'Do you think we should go straight home again?'

'Certainly not,' said Romeo. 'I'm not going to be pushed around!'

'Hallo,' said Noor. 'You haven't met each other, have you? This is Ming Chi from the first floor.'

Romeo made a being-sick noise.

'And this is Romeo.'

'You mean Harry!' shouted Lola.

'Oh, so that's Harry.' Ming Chi put his nose in the air.

Three cross-looking bears sat side by side in the sandpit and did not say a word.

'I've had enough of this,' said Noor. 'Shall we have a competition? The winner gets to marry Lola.'

'Yes,' cried Lola, 'a competition! I'll make up the questions myself.'

Ming Chi nodded.

'Goodie,' said Romeo.

'What is my favourite food?' said Lola.

'That's not a difficult question, bright Forget-me-not,' said Ming Chi. 'Someone as like a flower as you are must eat something to do with flowers. I am thinking of little stripy creatures which fly from flower to flower for you alone. They are gathering your favourite food: fragrant, golden honey. Am I right, Alpine Rose?'

'Wrong!' cried Lola, 'I don't like honey. Your turn, Harry.'

Romeo shrugged. 'I don't care for the nasty stuff myself, but she does: Lola-soup!'

'One-love to Harry,' said Lola. 'Question two: what would you say if you were asking me to go out with you?'

Ming Chi bowed and said: 'Flowering May, do you see the bright yellow moon in the sky? Can you smell the sweet scent of the rose blossom? Oh lovely Jasmine, come to my arms, and let us dance the whole night through . . .'

'I'd say: "Come on, ma'am, bop with the gang!"' said Romeo.

'That's what I thought, Harry,' said Lola, in an icy voice. 'Ming Chi won that one.'

'Gasbag bear!' said Romeo.

'I do not know what a gasbag bear is, but no doubt it is an insult,' said Ming Chi.

'You can bet your life it is!' shouted Romeo, clenching his fists. 'Come on, if you dare!'

'Put 'em up, Ming Chi,' cried Lola.

Romeo was bigger and stronger than Ming Chi. He grabbed Ming Chi by the throat and gave him a great box on the eye. That eye would turn purple soon, but with pandas you wouldn't notice.

Ming Chi swayed, grabbed Romeo by one paw and slung him through the air. Romeo fell on the hard stones and lay still. Noor and Lola ran to him.

'Romeo!' cried Lola, 'how do you feel? Does it hurt a lot?'

'Oh, my head!' groaned Romeo. 'Leave me, Lola. Go with the panda. He won you fair and square. I shall go and join the Foreign Legion.'

'I don't want that brute at all,' said Lola. 'I'm staying with you, my poor Romeo.'

84

She tied the scarf that Ming Chi had given her round Romeo's head.

'False Thistle!' cried Ming Chi. 'You have not kept your promise. I never want to see you again, Poisonous Poppy! Take me home at once, Noor.'

Noor picked up the angry panda. Before she ran back with him to the lower flat she saw Lola showering kisses on Romeo's wounded head.

Lola Disappears

Dad was lying full-length on the sofa.

'I'm tired out by all that wandering round the zoo,' he said. 'But I suppose you're not?'

'Not a bit,' said Christian. 'Do you know which animals I liked best, Noor's Dad? The crocodiles!'

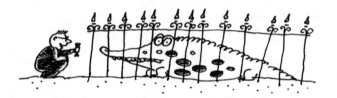

'The polar bears were much sweeter and more beautiful!' shouted Noor. 'Lola said so too, didn't you, Lola? Lola? Where are you? Lola's gone!'

'So's Romeo!' said Christian.

'They'll be lying about somewhere,' said Dad. 'Have another look in your room.'

Noor and Christian searched in Noor's room, in the passage, in the kitchen, in Dad's room and in the sitting-room. The bears were nowhere to be found.

Suddenly Christian gave a yell.

'We left them on the train! On the baggage rack!'

Noor jumped up. 'We must go to the station,' she said. 'Perhaps the train is still there.'

'The train has gone on,' said Dad. 'Calm down now. I'll ring the railway office. Someone may have found them and handed them in at the station.'

Dad telephoned the Lost Property Office, but the bears had not been found.

'They've been stolen!' sobbed Noor.

'I expect they're still on the train,' said Dad. 'I'll ring again tomorrow.'

'But I can't sleep without Romeo,' said Christian.

'And I can't sleep without Lola.'

'Stay and sleep with Noor, then. At least you will still have each other,' said Dad. 'But bath first!'

Dad put lots of bath foam in the water, but Noor and Christian sat in the foam with glum faces. After that they helped Dad to make up two mattress beds on the floor. Noor went off to get her duvet and pillow, and it was then that she spotted an envelope lying on the pillow. 'Noor' was written on the envelope.

'Dad, a letter! Read it out!'

Dad sat on the edge of the bed, opened the envelope and read:

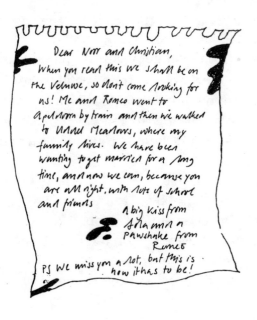

Dear Noor and Christian,
When you read this we shall be on the Veluwe, so don't come looking for us! Me and Romeo went to Apeldoorn by train and then we walked to Uddel Meadows, where my family lives. We have been wanting to get married for a long time, and now we can, because you are all right, with lots of school and friends

A big kiss from
Shamila n
Pawshake from
Romeo

PS We miss you a lot, but this is how it has to be!

Noor stamped the floor with rage.

'Lola must come back! I'm going to find her!'

'We'll take our car and drive to Veluwe. Now!' said Christian.

Dad hugged Noor and Christian tight. 'Lola doesn't want you to look for her,' he said. 'She

88

wants to live with Romeo and her family.'

'I think that's mean,' said Noor. 'She could get married here too.' She picked up her doll. 'You won't run away, will you, Josephina Katherina?'

'Course not,' said the doll. 'I'm not as stupid as that bear.'

Christian was holding the plush crocodile in his arms. He looked very gloomy.

'Now I'll never get to sleep,' he said.

'I know,' said Dad, 'write a letter back.'

Noor rushed to Dad's room and came back with paper and an envelope.

'Write!' she ordered. And Dad wrote:

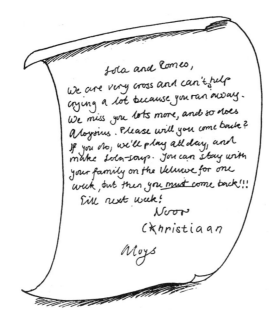

Sola and Romeo,
We are very cross and can't help
crying a lot because you ran away.
We miss you lots more, and so does
Aloysius. Please will you come back?
If you do, we'll play all day, and
make soda-soup. You can stay with
your family on the Veluwe for one
week, but then you must come back!!!
Till next week!
            Noor
        Christiaan
Moys

On the envelope Dad wrote:

> *To Lola and Romeo (Harry) Bear,*
> *Uddel Meadows*
> *The Veluwe*
> *Gelderland*
> *The Netherlands*

Noor stuck a stamp on the envelope and the three of them took the letter down to the letterbox.

'Now we have to wait a week,' said Noor.

 *Noor Two*

Five long nights passed. Josephina Katherina was a very nice doll, but she wasn't Lola. Then, on Saturday morning, there was a letter in their letterbox. Noor's name was on the envelope, so it must be a letter from Lola.

'Noor's Dad,' shouted Christian, 'come quickly!'

Noor tore open the envelope and Dad read out:

Dear Noor and Christian,

Thank you for your letter. Me and Romeo are married and would like to come back, but we can't now, because we have had triplets.

'Lola's got triplets!' screamed Noor.

So we are very busy. They are
called Noor, Christian and
Aloysius, after you. This is
a photo of us in front of our
new cave.

Kisses from Lola
and lots of good
wishes from my
husband Romeo

'She's called one of them after me!' said Dad.
'How nice!'

They looked at the photo. The bear who had
taken it was not a good photographer. When
Noor looked very hard indeed, she could
vaguely see two large and three small bears.

Noor and Christian made a beautiful big greetings card and Dad wrote 'Warmest Congratulations' under the picture.

They put the drawing in a big envelope, but before putting it in the letterbox, Noor secretly gave it a kiss.

One day Noor came home from school. She ran up the stairs to the top floor of the block of flats. And there, sitting in front of the door, was a little bear in a pink dress. There was a label pinned to the dress. Noor banged on the door.

Dad came running to open it and read out the note on the label:

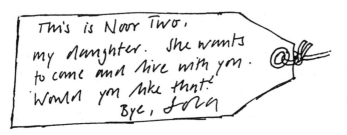

This is Noor Two, my daughter. She wants to come and live with you. Would you like that?
Bye, Lola

Noor looked at the little bear. She had a soft, yellow coat and brown eyes.

'So you are Noor Two,' she said.

'Who else would I be?' cried the little bear. 'Goose!'

Noor laughed. 'I can see it now,' she said. 'You are exactly like Lola!'